for Stan

Y0-AAF-599

Togetherness

*Five
Chambered
Heart*

Charles

FIVE CHAMBERED HEART

poems

Charles Greenleaf Bell

Charles G. Bell

Persea Books
New York

Persea Books
225 Lafayette Street
New York, N.Y. 10012

Library of Congress Cataloging in Publication Data
Bell, Charles Greenleaf.
  Five chambered heart.

  I. Title.
PS3503.E4313F5   1986   811'.54   86-2501
ISBN 0-89255-097-X
ISBN 0-89255-098-8 (pbk.)

Designed by Peter St. John Ginna

Set in Galliard by Keystrokes, Lenox, Massachusetts

Printed by BookCrafters, Chelsea, Michigan

First Edition

Acknowledgments

Some of the poems in this volume originally appeared in the following periodicals or anthologies:

The Annapolis Anthology; Approach; Center 12; The Chicago Sunday Tribune; Chicago Tribune Magazine; The College (Annapolis); Contemporary Poets of the English Language; The Desert Review; The English Leaflet; Epoch; Erotic Poetry; Hillsdale Review; The Indian Rio Grande; Journal of the Viola da Gamba Society of America; Ladies Home Journal; Modern Love Poems; New Mexican Review; New Letters; New Poems #2; The New York Times; The New York Times Book of Verse; Our Only Hope Is Humor; Out of War's Shadow; Paintbrush; Poetry; Puerto del Sol; Quarterly Review of Literature; The Rio Grande Sierran; St. John's Review; Saturday Review; A Seven Broadside; Thoreau Journal Quarterly; The View from the Top of the Mountain: Poems after Sixty; Washington and the Poet.

Consider the ways of clouds:
A cumulus by growing
Dissolves at the crown;
Shapes mingle and part—
Limbs that fold and unfold—
Glad in the play and dying
Io learned from Jove.

Praise age, sacred teacher
Of permissive desire,
A wantonness that smiles
As its claspings yield;
Blesses its own abroad
To quicken in other lives . . .
Nestlings I have loved,
Nestle with love's gods.

Contents

The poems of this book form twenty numbered waves which
move recurrently through five archetypal states of love:
LOVE simple; love narrowed, as in LUST; attached to things,
EARTH; perturbed or reversed, WASTE; transcended, SOUL.
Longer poems, imaging the same states, surround each sequence
of five such waves.

*Five
Chambered
Heart*

I

Five Chambered Heart

The first begins to beat like a drop of blood
On the egg-yolk of the world the fifth day
When vessels reach to guide the coded wave
Under brooding wings in the dark of LOVE.

A second cleaves the wish, one on one,
Mounts to spool and gender on its own:
Ruling reptiles upreared in a world
of electric LUST and cycad palm.

The third, of two and one, admits a space
Between self and other, EARTH-manifold,
Where love meanders the sensible,
And what it sees and meets with calls its own.

Four chambers pound with use gone wrong,
That all time, seas and saurians, beast and man
Kindle WASTE by everything we loved;
And lost the flower-turn from four to five.

Heart, infold again, world-fire infold,
SOUL cradled in a spiral swoon;
Still desire in cerements five-fold,
And do not ask of the all if up or down.

1

Rainbow

The passing caught and held—*percipio:*
An evening once in white-domed Mexico.

The sun, long set behind volcanic peaks,
Had flecked the clearing vault with salmon flakes.

Sunset was enough, a sky full;
But what we saw passed that: brighter than all,

A double rainbow, far up, out-flamed the cloud.
Twenty-five years together, and we stood

Almost in doubt, how loves so far gone
Crown a present less believed than known.

Litany of Women

I have forgotten the names of women I lay with in those days,
And yet they come across me, nameless distinctions:

One all flesh who beached from primal water
To be mounted in the ooze—sprawled, like saurians;

That lost empress who rode hard to the kill,
Then turned, still crouched, agape for the rearward monster;

Grower of grapes and grain, mother of tranquility,
Sun-burned, ox-eyed, in the Tuscan vineyard;

She whose purity, by London's sullied river,
Appeared a weeping babe tendering its pale flower;

You of the stately house, whose love reached through us,
To weave a custom, fireside, children, fine old fabrics;

And one who tore all fabrics, by Easter starlight
Praying, in fierce humility, to be God's mother;

And that high lonely thing who calls all hearts forever,
Proud on the tower, over towns and beached ships blazing.

Rainsong of Fish and Birds

A long drought. In the heat this afternoon,
Unaccountably, the birds
Begin to sing.

I go with mask and snorkel to the pond. Plumb.
Fish come round me: black bass, goggle-eye, brim
Flowing and retreating, expectant among
The water-weed. When I come up to breathe,
The interface is dimpled with white spume
Rustling on the water; thunder shakes the trees;
The birds are singing in a gust of rain:

How cause and wish,
Foreknowledge, chance and deed
Rustle around us dark and luminous as rain.

High Tension

My life in strange places.
Night. I climb a bank,
Try a short-cut through some trees.

The hum in the dark increasing.

(In New York yesterday
I saw my crazy Charlotte
Penned up, ranting.)

They loom in dim light, fenced with warning,
Ringed tails upended, barbed

Hornets, buzzing.

(A jet zooms over; somewhere fire is falling.)

I think these Martian wasps hatched our civilization;
And I go past as she, past a policeman,
Muttering against the curse, steeled against the sting.

The Voice of the Chambered Fire

Moments, when the heart
Fills with unconnected burning,
A black-body rounding
On itself, when mind,
Almost part sharer in the fire,
Lays the treasured word-hoard on the hearth:
"How we two leaning in a certain window"
And "Come to the window, sweet is . . ."

Pours on memory's oil:
The bee in the blossom, beyond the castle,
Over the slopes of Tyrol.
Remember? The songs of Wolkenstein?
When our youth sang with the world?
Though all that birth of love
Leaned to a century of wars, the timeless
Twisting of the human child—

And we play the record maybe:
"mit lieber zal . . . das in dem wald erklingt."
Knowing in the darkness nothing moves outward,
All things return on the windowless
Close burning (if through the glass window there
The blade-thin shape of a moon puts off its cloud),
The chambered fire, that murmurs as it dies:
"Forbid that any love should doubt its own."

2

Wake Robin

To see the summer stars, Scorpion, Lyre,
The clustered Milky Way—with Venus now—
Risc before winter dawn,
Brings a softer breath down mountain snows.

I, Hiem, and you June: what glints of love
At the dawn rising of your summer stars
Over my snow fields,
Stir, sweet shimmerer, these April airs?

Dogwood and Flowering Judas

Cornel, a Florentine profile,
Snow-maiden
Quatrefoil dawn-flower;

Redbud, Venetian putana,
Spilling the
Wine of noon's orgies;

In the garden of the heart—
God said—
Let them bloom together.

Giant Spruce

To climb that liquidly resilient up the air,
To take fixed and swaying all year the wind and rain,
To point branch over branch the sky-bone of the spire
And trail for the nurture of light sun-terraces of green,
Through centuries to unfold the template we are—
Dreams the earth-conqueror as he kindles fire.

The White Room

A high window, a white room.
Paper, pen, table, chair.
Of the longest life, half is gone.
Cars on the street below are a blur.

Strange to write and no one to read.
There was my mother; her wits are with God.
That will save postage. Journals, friends
Answer with smiles or blank returns.

To work as if the working were a trade,
Knowing it will not leave the windowed room,
Knowing, almost desiring. Another fall
Turns to winter, gray-brown under cloud.

Is the vigil of the word
At a cradle or a tomb?
And how to work the will of God
With God alone, in the white room?

Resonance of Towers

Tonight in the lighted tower
I have outwatched the Bear.

Think of Dante in banishment
Climbing another's stairs by candlelight,

Collins in the clouded hut,
Rock-walled Jeffers, embattled Yeats.

Rats with electrodes in their heads
Jump on the treadle for a charge.

The night web of soul in the world
Leans from tower to tower.

3

A Wife Gathers

Is it for one
Such meanings stir
To elations
Of despair
You walk dry fields
In the last sun
Gathering blue thistles
Hedged with thorn?

Dancing Mother

The palm shack bellies—
Strings and gourds—
Mother and all are dancing;

While frogs from vines
And flame trees take it up:
"Coqui, co-co-co-qui."

Sweep breadfruit breasts
Down laurel hair; under
The mangoes hanging weave your loins,

Woman of the night and frogs,
Ishtar, mother of flesh,
Gaea, mother of gods.

The Berlin Titian

Where Venus in the lap of flesh,
Subdued by music, turns her thighs,
The lover plays; only his eyes
Pursue those generous valleys, flank and breast.

But in a landscape broad as dream,
Brown fields and mountains in dim light,
The curtained carriage of his thought
Drives to a stable, drawn by a plunging team.

Being, on its downward course,
Delays in music, delegates the act;
Love unentered is the root
Whose flower is beauty, whose seed is force.

Termites

A friend writes from the temperate zone:
He has a fourth child, a golden girl.

Through unscreened windows
Termites swarming
Drift to the light;
Dropping wings,
White worms on the table,
Pursue and mate;
Then eat into the books
Blotting the word.

Procreation wraps us like a spider's web.
To my friend, what blessings of the occasion?

Inwardness

Close your eyes against the sun.
In the fire-vault, look, a man—
Fearless—among flaming lions.

[10]

4

From Height and Silence

How shall I, who
From childhood have lived
In the recklessness
You fear, know what you have
To forget, what to forgive?

But that we being as Blake
Said on earth a little space
Have learned how saints kiss
In the Angelic Brother's
Paradise.

Who will believe
Their innocence
Is lack of touch?
They have put off the weight
Of shame, not flesh.

I do not trust desire,
Much less regret.
At home in love as in air
I wait. Incommunicables
Why confess?

Eurydice

Orion and the Dog are lifting
Over the east; the dew has fallen.
We have come late
To bivouac under the stars.

I see you at dawn among the early dead
Who walk by the river on the other shore,
And far off and cold to us
Are our love-glances.

Dunghill Harbinger

Only the poor keep roosters.

In the dark before the dawn
From every moonvine porch
And shanty ridgepole breaks
The raw confirmatory cry.

The suburbs of the rich are silent.

Chicago Twenty Years After

The city always taller over the shore;
The sirens of its promise heavier;
I almost caught in the dream rush as before.

Ask the manikin whose mythic hair
Slogans a costly tweed: "Was the Western star
We pledged with life, tinsel as you are?"

Smiles lewd, smiles last: "What Promethean lure
Set your soul to sell, in a mortgaged store,
That three-piece suit of freedom, profit, war?"

Silver-Sable

On the lake pier, at the end of winter,
Under a moon of mist, trailing my feet,
I look back to the city of my hate.

Lids half close; through tears and lashes,
That moonlit shattered world goes silver-sable:
Lanes and extensions of star-drift work

Live cross-hatchings in the spaceless
Dark. "The eye rubbed," says Plotinus,
"Sees the light it contains—truest seeing."

5

Polly's Winter Tree

A stone lintel like a grave . . .
I remember leaves
She gathered casually,
As over a battleground
A goddess of death and return
Stoops for the noblest slain—

To be pressed between book-
leaves until the dark
Of the year, when at her
Voice and hand, the russet
And purple and tawny leaves,
Shaken from their graves—

Maple, tulip, linden,
Flame red, umber, black-veined,
Fledged to a beech limb,
With lost fall fill the room;
And I come where Polly Persephone
Is love in her garden caves.

Encore

Marianne:
        I swear, if Eve seduced Adam to eat the fruit
(Or Lilith—to whatever gauds she lured him),
It was not by brow or breast or the dear hoarded
Slopes of belly, but by the tongued and breathing flute
Of song. Witness yourself, just old enough to be
My second daughter; and when you sing that song by Schubert,
Your lips parted for the secret savor
Of lost romantic passion, you so confound me,
I forget wives, loves, whores, daughters, granddaughters,
To lie in the falls of your Lydian laughter.

[13]

If ever poet-lover plunged
Off the deep end, it is the drowned
                    Yours forever,

                              Charles

Doctrine of Signatures

Through entropic December of shifting total fog,
Blurs to the branch of the barely discernible apple tree
A condensing shape: scarlet, black-crested, tail-perked, winged.

Whatever cleaves the blank and nebular immensity
With the self-proclamation of a bounded thing, name-bearing,
Jocund, smug, gives the password—one with me.

A Fly Thrown into the Fire

The black body shrinks and hisses
        Fringed with light—
What stretched the neck, what preened
        Head and wings,
Changed to incandescence—
        All flesh grass
In the hands of the living God.

Man

Two, subconscious of each
Other, one waking
While the other sleeps.

To reach out and touch
The double above our waking,
The one, who sleeps.

II

Wave Plots in Space and Time

1

Two loves have brought me to a cold March shore:
The old of ocean and another new:
Gray eyes paired on the breaking gray;
Lips as changeful as the sea.

Tell those who love you, when they look at you,
To leave possession; for your face will shift
With banished Eve from smiling into grief.

Like sandpipers, up and down with the wash,
I follow the wave-play of those lips.

2

From the windowed house Atlantic day
Renews, you with me, flower-gowned.
After thirty years to watch the dawn rose
Throw petals on the waves. We have no better
Teachers than the gods: ocean, sun
Squander tides of unconditioned love.

For kind, who cares—and who cares not?

3

Grass stems mark the turn of day
By the shadows' conjugate curves;
Wave-concaves, toward noon, focus sun.
Small ones, down the beach, crack musket fire;
The thunder of the great, carried higher,
Thins to a whisper as the surf shoals in.

On the strand of now time's motion rides:
Wind in the grass over migrant dunes,
Sand-ripples shadowed from the low sun.

The most ephemeral most of all endures.

[15]

4

Motorbikes barrel the strand. Oil slicks;
Surf brown; sledged foam. Washed no more
In the limitless, illimitable blue.
To float a dream
Of lawns and houses down the Main Line
We slag earth's ocean to a dying pool.
Good times end it sooner; give us good times.

To ride the love-surge of your youth
I could almost pioneer another westward death.

5

The finite effluent takes the sky.
Change rounds on itself, the lift and lean
Crashing always to a shoreward spill,
Restless as the molecular sliding fives
By which (some say) the fluid state obtains.

We ride face backward on the time train.
Hours and miles of distance clacking to more,
Every paired Bosch bubble turns to dream,
Whether of earth or woman.
                                        Cry the other
Sea: spermatic tongues of flame, wider
Than the lost, more changeable—unchanged.

6

Leaving Bavaria

Gentian waters down from snow,
Restless, as my thoughts to you,
Probe a space of temporal valleys
For the rock-pass of solace.

The eye to see can only scan,
Fingers wander for the form;
Face of absence, foundling, come,
Weep the landscape of return.

Sand and Snow

You lie on dune sand.
How sacredly
Your bare hip swells
The air—hill
Of my desire, cool
In the grass-blowing wind.

.   .   .

Snow falls. Lost
From your love
I have the taste
Of death under my tongue.

Silver Lining

Give me a hill, that when it rains
Shows some far-off corner of the scene—

Mountains lighted by the sun
With all the cloud-washed air between—

Sandia, Jemez, Taylor, through the veil,
To keep one life-illusion real.

Fly Bait

Stung with sweat and flies
I strip for the rock pool. Dive.
When I come up rock-clean,
Black swarms on my clothes
Flout me. Like all the world's fools—
Sold on the leavings of a man.

Sursum Corda

In cold night
The crooked log
Spouts fire.
No more asked
Of death-loves than this:
That punk at midnight
Bleed like stars in space—
How fiercely vindicated
The earth that wrings our hearts.

7

Engendered in the Eyes

"You are old;
  Forego the love
  Of women and the world."

"To the world
  Old and loveless
  I quit claim;

"But to women hold
  While their eyes
  In mine

"Plead the world
  Old and loveless
  And love unclaimed."

Alpha and Omega

She turns for shame, her
Ripe Omega
Mirrored in the water

Striptease of the pool, turn
Again, reveal
The sacred Alpha, cuneiform.

Heroes

A pair of gray mallards,
Almost invisible,
Move in the distance;

Only their ripples
Catch the sunset;
And those birds—

Light into darkness—
Ride the still world
Ignorantly glorified.

Victor-Victim

Read your own SONGS:
The publishable flash;
Better these, hopeless—

Dystrophic youth
Crutching to class,
El Greco eyes—

Manikin world, to fling
Once in your teeth
A statement like that.

Pool of Tao

I waited the fulness of time.
As sunset deepened
The wind died.
In the hush the pool
Was an iris of trees
Fringing a sky—

Motionless, until
A flight of geese passed over;
Then I heard the sound
Of water, a stream
That falls to the pool,
Lingers, and falls away.

When the geese were gone
The sky gave over
The motion received;
But mine was full,
Holding flight and water,
The arrow and the wheel.

8

Aubade

All night I have kept you waking
  In the wreathed unrest of love;
We have seen the gray moon streaking
  The warm hills of home,
The long moonlight probing
  The fringed lake and grove.

Now day is breaking
  And day birds are shrill;
Reason comes creating
  In the blind depths of the will;
And to the world of making
  I follow the day's spell.

But you, my love, will shade you
  Deep in the sepia grove.
Sleep, my soul's soft shadow;
  I would not have you move,
Until the moon and I shall wake you
  To the wreathed unrest of love.

Banana

Unexpectedly, from the highest shoot, a huge
Thing detaches itself, leaving the sheath
Slowly like a stallion's appalling member,

Curling, purpling, thrusting out an emergent
Flower that lifts from day to day petals
Like loin cloths, revealing the genitalia:

Enlarging fingers of banana capped with cream,
Dropping nectar, to which small queenbirds fly, and sing
The shocking abandon of fertile and phallic bloom.

Barn Swallow

A swallow skims low over the field,
Turning and darting as insects rise.
I see the blue back, orange breast, forked tail;
Pursue the motions, the bank, the dive,
The swerve in flight that nabs swerving flies.
He sees me also, bends his course
To skirt my presence, flutters, cries.

I like that fluttering; I only guess
At what he likes, beyond his prey.
I do not take the invisible world on trust;
Probabilities remain, and this is probable:
The flight of his outwardness, the stance of mine,
Harbor like visitants, some angel I,
Banking in timelessness, intrinsic, free.

On the Shore of Birth

"Odysseus, stern guard,
  Put up the sword;
  I am the prophet;
  Let my tongue
  Blossom in speech."

I wake, my mouth filled
With the salt reek of blood.

Stranger

From towering darkness,
Flash and thunder;
The lights go off together.

The old woman
Understands a moment
Then forgets, gropes
From lamp to lamp
To flick them on,
Bewildered
Calls the cat.

(To bring the years'
Stray kittens from the storm.)

A door slams in a gust,
Trees brush the window,
Rain in sheets goes
Solid on the screens.

She trips and stands smiling,
Lost but not worried
(It is we
Who draw back in fear);
The smile on her lips,
She calls into the darkness
Further than drowned light:

"Here Kitty, Kitty, Kitty;
Come Kitty, Kitty;
Come Kitty."

9

The Fire

The fire was slow kindling; it was damp wood.
Twice I rose, to mend it, from your side;
Stirred the wet sticks and blew the smoldering ends.
Then in the cold night clearing of the wood,
We two, not young, wet with time's worse rains,

Forgot the fire; until suddenly it was there,
Point kindling point to take us by surprise;
A majesty of light, a living blaze,
That sent up sparks to coil across the sky,
Earth's poor matter assaulting the dark.

On this ground, the shore where we are bred,
We watched the lattice of transfigured wood
Slough films of gray ash and renew its glowing,
And in the clear space of the dew-cold forest,
Saw the last sparks waver among the stars.

Girl Walking

Here comes a girl so damned shapely
Loungers stop breathing. Conceive how subtly
She works those hips. She is all sex, she knows it.
Lace shows the bubs; she is proud of notice—
Head high, back arched, long braids, wide crupper—
Walks like dancing, calls the gods to tup her.

Her mother goes before, full as a tick,
A trundling hill of flesh, a breeding sack,
Swollen with stoking of all appetites.
She stirs her buttocks too, but not to our delight.

Body of flame, how can you stroll
With such impulsive beauty, admired by all,
Your destiny waddling before you down the road?

November Tower

The big wind rattles the glass of the eight-sided tower. It has
Blown down all our fall, all the late lingering of those leaves.
Bring the fur-collared coat, castoff of a hunting friend;
Bring the fleece-lined brogans, lug table and chair
Here where the pale sun slants through southwest panes.
On all four quarters the stripped expanse of cold-shrunken land
Circles this self-center. Bite down on that now. Until time
Smiles, swing—a bulldog at the focus of the bare earth-wheel.

Pterodactyl

I sang the vine of beauty on the slopes
Of terror, hungry for reaches
Of the reptile seaways—Niobrara. . .

In despair even of cleaning the bottles,
Cans, wrecked cars from our own back yard,
We take wing and glorious
Rain fire and poison on far-off
Margins of the world. . .

We chose it in theory:
Night after night in prophecies of flame
Acclaimed the world-commitment
Where it seemed our greatness to burn;
Hated the funk of reaction,
Withering earth's call to globaloney.

Now we wake to the Midas touch of fire,
Where do we go to be human again?

Rose of Sharon

Women I have seen ripe as fruit
In the green hills on the low horizon
When the voice of the turtle was heard in our land,

Withered in the pantry; and the men of my youth
Gristle and fat. Who calls from the waste country:
Like a roe or hart upon the mountain of spices?

Yet Shulamite-Magdalen at the dying fire,
A crumpled bone-bag, sings against the darkness:
Until day break and the shadows flee away.

And at the deathbed of a loved woman
I have found the last silence charred with sighs:
Stay me with flagons, for I am sick of love.

How all these cold days of the weeping spring,
Crouched at the fire, this gaunt flesh sings:
Rose of Sharon. . .as the lily among thorns.

10

Deus Fortior Me

Beyond your husband at the church service
Your folded hands and face raised
Preach the greater law: to find a way,

Gothic, tender, total, dark, and
Skyward, as when flesh possessed
Breathes "I love you" in its rutting thrust.

Be Secret

Is love simple? What if mothers
Come to kindness lifting conscience
Gownlike to the touch of lovers?

Is love partial? Have not husbands
Won the glory of their wives
By the toss of a girl's thighs?

And who knows if everybody loves best
Where the need of love is least
And Eros like Agape gives itself?

Two Scales

For the Greeks the natural succession was Orpheus descending;
Gold into Iron; Phlegethon, ground of passion;
Post and lintel of tragic song.

Our scale rises, Gothic vaultings,
The grave that moults the angelic butterfly:
The third is love, the seventh pain, the diapason fire.

Echo

Nearing the Halloween that nears three score,
Century of our ruin, quit the town;
Past pinyon hills spider-webbed with roads,
Thread Arroyo Moro up Atalaya's bowl.

Cliffs of Precambrian metamorphic gneiss
Mottled and folded with dark Vishnu schist. . .
More than old trees and almost as much as stars,
You have always loved and hankered after rock.

If then the amorphous jelly of the tongue
Take voice: What seeking? WHAT ITS OWN? Does not
This cleft gorge of the flawed earth, weatherings
Of pink and grey, give back the answer: STONE?

Dark Trail

Bare your feet, old man, that once
On midnight mountains, for a wife—

Yours or another's erring—
Searched the dark

(How love's lost follies burn
Remembered youth, as if desired);

Dark again and mountains,
The worn touch of the ground—

With creased feet bare, Tiresias,
Grope the deeper trail.

III

Archetypes with Translations

1

By Victor Hugo, past eighty years old
Ave Dea: moriturus te salutat—A Judith Gautier

La mort et la beauté sont deux choses profondes
Qui contiennent tant d'ombres et d'azur qu'on dirait
Deux soeurs également terribles et fécondes
Ayant la même énigme et le même secret.

Ô femmes, voix, regards, cheveux noirs, tresses blondes,
Brillez, je meurs! Ayez l'eclat, l'amour, l'attrait,
Ô perles que la mer mêle à ses grandes ondes,
Ô lumineux oiseaux de la sombre forêt!

Judith, nos deux destins sont plus près l'un de l'autre
Qu'on ne croirait, à voir mon visage et le vôtre;
Tout le divin abîme apparaît dans vos yeux,

Et moi, je sens le gouffre étoilé dans mon âme;
Nous sommes tous les deux voisins du ciel, madame,
Puisque vous êtes belle et puisque je suis vieux.

Hail Goddess: We Who Are to Die Salute You— To Judith Gautier

Death and beauty are two somber loves,
As deep in blue and shade as if to say:
Two sisters, alike fecund and destructive,
Bearing the burden of one mystery.

Loves, voices, looks, tresses dark and fair,
Be radiant; for I die. Hold light, warmth, solace—
You pearls the sea rolls in waves up the shore,
You birds that nestle, luminous, in the forest.

Judith, our destinies are nearer kin
Than one might think to see your face and mine.
The abyss of all opens in your eyes—

The same starred gulf I harbor in my soul.
We are neighbors of the sky, and for this cause,
That you are beautiful and I am old.

2

Goethe: *Selige Sehnsucht*

Sagt es niemand, nur den Weisen,
Weil die Menge gleich verhönet:
Das Lebendige will ich preisen,
Das nach Flammentod sich sehnet.

In der Liebesnächte Kühlung,
Die dich zeugte, wo du zeugtest,
Überfällt dich fremde Fühlung,
Wenn die stille Kerze leuchtet.

Nicht mehr bleibest du umfangen
In der Finsternis Beschattung,
Und dich reisset neu Verlangen
Auf zu höherer Begattung.

Keine Ferne macht dich schwierig,
Kommst geflogen und gebannt,
Und zuletzt, des Lichts begierig,
Bist du, Schmetterling, verbrannt.

Und solang du das nicht hast,
Dieses: Stirb und werde!
Bist du nur ein trüber Gast
Auf der dunklen Erde.

Sacred Lust

Tell the wise; the many lour,
And make ignorance their shame;
Say I praise the living power
That hungers for a death of flame.

Love-nights breed us as we breed:
In the candlelighted cool,
Feel the gates of dark go wide
For the moulting of the soul.

From its woven bed of shadows
Mere enclosure falls away:
Love spreads new wings to the meadows
Of another mating play.

Tireless, upward; spaces dwindle;
Nothing hems declared desire;
God is light and light will kindle,
And the moth wings leap in fire.

Know, until you learn to weave
Each flame-dying into breath,
Everywhere you haunt the grave
Of the shadowed earth.

3

Petrarch XI, *in morte di Madonna Laura*

Se lamentar augelli, o verdi fronde
mover soavemente a l'aura estiva,
o roco mormorar di lucide onde
s'ode d'una fiorita e fresca riva,

là 'v'io seggia d'amor pensoso e scriva;
lei che 'l ciel ne mostrò, terra n'asconde,
veggio et odo et intendo, ch'ancor viva
di sì lontano a' sospir miei risponde:

"Deh perché innanzi 'l tempo ti consume?"
mi dice con pietate: "a che pur versi
degli occhi tristi un doloroso fiume?

Di me non pianger tu, che' miei dì fersi
morendo eterni, e nell' eterno lume,
quando mostrai di chiuder, gli occhi apersi."

After Laura's Death

If birds' lament, green leaves' or tendrils' stir
To the soft sighing of the air of summer,
Or through the wave-wash at the petalled shore
Of a clear stream, crystal's liquid murmur
Sound, where I sit bowed to the forest floor—
Her, whom heaven showed and earth now covers,
I see and hear and know, as if the power
Of her live voice responded from afar:

"Why do you spend yourself before your years?"
She asks in pity. "Or wherefore and for whom
Pour the wasting river of your tears?
You must not weep for me. My life became,
Dying, eternal; and to eternal skies,
The dark, that seemed to close them, cleared my eyes."

4

Catulli Carmina, XXIX

Quis hoc potest uidere, quis potest pati,
nisi impudicus et uorax et aleo,
Mamurram habere quod Comata Gallia
habebat uncti et ultima Britannia?
cinaede Romule, haec uidebis et feres?
et ille nunc superbus et superfluens
perambulabit omnium cubilia,
ut albulus columbus aut Adoneus?
cinaede Romule, haec uidebis et feres?
es impudicus et uorax et aleo.
eone nomine, imperator unice,
fuisti in ultima occidentis insula,
ut ista uestra diffututa mentula
ducenties comesset aut trecenties?
quid est alid sinistra liberalitas?
parum expatrauit an parum elluatus est?
paterna prima lancinata sunt bona,
secunda praeda Pontica, inde tertia
Hibera, quam scit amnis aurifer Tagus:
nunc Galliae timetur et Britanniae.
quid hunc malum fouetis? aut quid hic potest
nisi uncta deuorare patrimonia?
eone nomine, urbis opulentissime
socer generque, perdidistis omnia?

Catullus, 29. Attack on Caesar for his favorite Mamurra

The man who can face this, the man who can take it,
Is whored himself, a drunk, a swindler. Mamurra
Laps the fat of crested Gaul and farthest Britain.
Pansied Romulus, you see this thing, you take it?
How he struts his way through everybody's bedroom,
Like a white dove, a white-skinned soft Adonis—
Pansied little Roman, you take it in, you bear it?
You are like him then, as drunk, as whored a swindler.
And was it for this, Rome's only great general,
You conquered the remotest island of the West,
To feed this screwed-out tool of yours, Mamurra?
See him spend, twenty or thirty million? First were
His own estates, then the loot of Pontus, then of Spain—
Hear Tagus, the gold-bearing river. They say the Gauls
And Britains fear him? And you love the mongrel? Both
Of you, Caesar, Pompey? While he swills oil of patrimony?
For this, like in-laws, father and son,
You have sluiced wealth and all of the world-city.

5

San Juan de la Cruz
Canción de la subida del Monte Carmelo

En una noche oscura,
con ansias en amores inflamada,
oh dichosa ventura!
salí sin ser notada,
estando ya mi casa sosegada.

A escuras y segura
por la secreta escala, disfrazada,
o dichosa ventura!
a escuras, en celada,
estando ja mi casa sosegada.

En la noche dichosa,
en secreto, que nadie me veía,
ni yo miraba cosa,
sin otra luz ni guía,
sino la que en el corazón ardía.

Aquesta me guiaba
mas cierto que la luz de mediodía,
adonde me esperaba
quien yo bien me sabía,
en parte donde nadie parecía.

Oh noche, que guiaste,
oh noche amable mas que el alborada,
oh noche, que juntaste
Amado con amada,
amada en al Amado transformada!

En mi pecho florido,
que entero para él solo se guardaba,
allí quedó dormido,
yo le regalaba,
y el ventalle de cedros aire daba.

El aire del almena,
cuando ya sus cabellos esparcía,

The Ascent of Mount Carmel

In the dark of night
With love inflamed
By luck, by chance
I rose unseen
From the house hushed in sleep.

Safe in the dark
By a secret stair
My luck, my chance
And night for a veil
I stole from the house of sleep.

By chance of night
By secret ways
Unseeing and unseen
No light, no guide
But the flames that my heart gave—

Led by those rays
Surer than day
I came where one waits
Who is known to me
In a place none seemed to be.

Night that guides
Purer than dawn
Night that joins
Lover and loved
And the loved into Lover changed.

In my flowered heart
That is only his
He lay in sleep
Lulled by the breeze
The fanning of my cedars gave.

Down turrets that air
With hand serene

con su mano serena,
en mi cuello hería
y todos mis sendidos suspendía.

Quedéme y olvidéme,
el rostro recliné sobre el Amado,
cesó todo, y dejéme,
dejando mi cuidado
entre las azucenas olvidado.

As it stirred in his hair
Gave my throat a wound
That took all sense away.

I ceased, I was gone
My face to his own
All passed away
Care and all thrown down
There among the lillies where I lay.

11

The Place

Where moss banks the stream
His running stopped;
Palms catch the temples'
Fluttering.

The nearer to dying we are
In the forest of loss,
The more wish makes us
A nest of wings.

Two Families

In rain-forest Chiapas, at the table of Chang,
American Gothic exhibits right from wrong.
The Iowa mission sends this virtuous couple
To demonstrate imperatives of the moral:
Hobbled, who grazed and scratched together
Thirty years without breaking a tether,
Exhort through lips like a pursed-up bag
(Categorical sabotage)
Our old forest Maya with his child-wife and child
And his old wives and children—and look, how they smile!

Day of Cambodia

Always far off, the soft assurance: the first
Note tentative, a second rising, in question
Or alarm, three then of comfort, breathed, subsiding.

Thunder darkens over the woods of error
Where I walk listening, slow to fathom
The five-fold tones of a dove's covenant.

Organic Spectra in Interstellar Dust

When we drive up a long road slanting a little toward the sky,
I see beyond the clouds space sowed with worlds.

Over all civilizations we flushed and disinfected—
Wishful eyes on progress.

Punctual—disaster kindling in our bounty—
How life's fierce radicals,

Hydroxyl, methane, cyanogen, ammonia,
Sow the stellar void with wishful poisons.

World-Cave

I light the torch
And lift it to inscribe in smoke
My curse, my warning on the wall.

Is it rock crystal
Shining? Gold mosaics? Shapes
I have known: Cross, Lyre, Crown!

12

The Pool

There is a valley in that forest
Green with siftings off the leaves;
Water with a low sound down the stone
Gathers to silence, where a pool
Floats the lights and shadows of the grove.

In the wavering, I cannot tell
Which is better: if sight alone
Surface where leaf-shadows move,
Or body plunge into the deepest
Sway and lapping of the water's hold.

Only from every day's appearance
I take the path down to that pool;
Watch, where the slow drop from the stone,
In its trembling tear-shape mirrors
Two forms laced in a forest dark as love.

Housemaid's Knee

("When he was live and had his feeling,
She was on her back and he was kneeling")

How have I contracted housemaid's knee?
By devout kneeling to housemaids.
Schismatic loves, womb-liberators,
If you overturn the service at that altar,
If may ease my chronic malady.

Micturitions

From the flickering dark of the mezzanine
I reach a porcelain room marked MEN.
In mercury light I see as strange
The stream that was me, from my flesh,
Leave me, this seeing nothingness.

* * *

I water in the moonlight on the grass.
My drops, globed on grass,
Moon back at me—delight's
Deliquescent light.

Father of Lies

Paid again, peace talker,
The tax that bombs and flames.

You enter the bedroom door,
Your shadow on the wall.

The door slams behind
Blotting you out.

Shut in the dark
With the shape you have become.

Kindled at How Many Hearths

Music, always reaching in the flow
A seat of permanence. . .

The hermit crab, distinguished
Less by solitude than wandering,
Readiness
Among shells of a beach pile
To go on shifting ground.
I do not understand the juncture
Between timelessness and time, the hunger
For an actual home, requiring homelessness.
Being of that foreclosure, I take it
Like bread and wine; I call it incarnation.

. . . Listen to the viols:
Indwelling soul, homing, down the shadows.

13

Te, Dea

The well
That floats the leaf
And flower
Drowning them;

The flame
That folds itself
In flaming
And is still;

Well-flame
Where all spirals
Leaf-dying
Fire-renewed.

Houghmagandie

Even the Romans in the decadence
That loamed the fallen world with monuments
Of their gloom, and when the bitterness of sex surprised them,
Sought it, loved it, prized it.

Out of fabulous crypts of the Dark Ages
Issue nameless voices,
Avowed monks on their knees declining
To the dear socket of a girl's inturning.

Sanctimonius Puritans
Warmed beds with bundling; Victorian
Dames veiled under bustles of silence the same fesses,
Smooth, indented, thighs spread for caressing.

Body, naked, cloven, supple, swaying—
Here, where the great cloud waits at

The sun's horizon, shall we not mate and slumber,
Our foldings wreathed again on the leaves of Indian summer?

Windowed Habitations

East, over the water, nothing but trees,
Green shadowing nature. At sunset suddenly
A light appears, a torch, a star,
Another sun, pouring through dark leaves.

We are leaf-shadowed here; give us reflections:
Something not ours to image, that over water,
Someone, far off, will say: "Surely
That is one of soul's windowed habitations."

Gloomy Dis

It was not in ignorance: again and again
We mounted time's slope; though time
Had given proof romantics rifle virgins—
This round of sea and land soul so loved
That eyes still westward take through tears
The heave and crashing of those sullied waves.
To have her young again—Proserpina.

Gnomic

The night each sows
A furrow of death
In the field of stars
Who calls?

*I am nothing
But one with the one
That makes the nothing
All.*

14

Bleibe der Flamme Trabant
(Stefan George: *Hold to the Flame*)

Where they rose from the woods by the water
    she painted the bay and shore

Caught in a flagrance of loss that made
    the land all fire—

Orion's burning sea, love's old nebula.

Half a world away, he frames it
    on the wall

In a rainbow of tears, always earth's
    water sign

And airy cry at dying: trust the fire.

Two Centers

Full-face! Arms spread, legs spanned!
Sex marks the center of Vitruvian man.

Only from above—vertical view—
Head focuses our radial play;

And that blind worm, groping below,
Comic appendage, points one way.

Western Dragon

Lights, along the tidal reaches
Dark—cities—I see you lovelier
And lonelier than ever in our days

Of hope, your beauty rooted
In your loneliness.

Dark by day, clouding
The embayments of your streams,
Breeding hutches of our troubled souls,
At night you constellate a coil of flame
Along the roads of water.

And we, airborne through night,
Catch by the bay the renewed
Dragon of fire. The old snake
Casts his skin, that every scale
Spangles in our tears.

World Choice

Our freedom death, our life-road
Tyranny... Soul, spinning itself out
In matter, plant, beast, bird—
Was every turning point as desperate?

When nature took the habit of fixed law,
Attraction deadened into gravity—
Did all stand then as now in such love-doubt
Where the blind longing would lead?

Resonance

When I see the world reduced to sky
And rock and a bare spacing of trees,
Perspective rhythms choir in standing waves.

Love does not count on man;
In space and time extension weaves
The celebration of its magnitudes.

15

Da unser zweier Bette was

You, smiling from the ground, a Chartres angel fallen—
Mothwing lids on eyes preternaturally blue—
Are you ingredient in the secret landscape?
Or must I wake some day, the sun as now a furnace
In the gum trees, this moss-bed crushed beside me,
And know you for the phantom seen since childhood:
Fair-haired Sainte Modeste, Queen Cunegunde, smiling Uta?

Baby Blue-eyes

Paired with eyes as luminous as blue
That break in glances over a swelling sea,
A student stands before me, lips inquiring:
May her thesis be of love, on which she is knowledgable.

    Sight swims with blue:
    Where waves crest white
    On purple, there the reef
    Down swinging fans unfolds
    The coral of its caves.

    Once we go far enough
    Into the element, fear
    Turns to desire; the green
    Eel withdraws, we follow
    Into the deeper water.

"No doubt," I tell her, "that will be satisfactory.
Relate it if you can to Penelope and Calypso."
How peerlessly her swaying leaves the room,
And leaves it swaying, like a tide-pool, blue.

Cañada Corrales

Sacred, in dry country, every stream.
This, from Atalaya, down a black sill
Of outcrop marble, carved at the rim
A bowl for flesh to bathe, in Eden's truth:

Chest-deep, worn for two, female, male,
Chastened in cool water and close stone,
Rippled through the clear to harvest miles
Of rock and canyon, sky and valley pine.

Until a new buyer made a cement dam
For a swimhole, crazed the gradient;
The first flash-flood brimmed rock and all
With gravel, where shoal water slides.

Forcing nature is our life and death:
Oedipus plows the mother, to their pain;
A risk with love and knowledge; wanting both,
Defiance flung to the boomerang.

Weed Farm

Take a truck-jack after rain,
Wrap the corded stalk around,
Heave back, levering to a ton;
As if a devil groaned
    "Karrunk"—
Feet of dark bull pizzle jimmies out.

Green Vermont. Kinnell from Plaquemine:
Clubbed and jailed. I fling
The burdock, twist the next, heaving
For the death-groan—Ah—
    "Karrunk"—
As mad as wrong or right to purge the earth.

[52]

Love of Number

ONE

The point alone.
Dilate it (birdcall, waves in a pond,
Circle and sphere, in the gravity of oneness, raindrops, stars)
Cleaves an in from out, other from same,
Self-reflecting

TWO

Since every actual round
Stretches on some yoke, oblate dividing star,
Breeds the antinomy of poles. Fix on the void between—
In turbulence the axis mounts a thrust
Bisecting: pyramid of

THREE

Timaeus' flame.
From there to four asks toil, vertex
Split apart; asks skill, to draw them equally, balance the post
And lintel temple of the year, Roma Quadrata,
Circumscribed

FOUR

Too perfect.
Reason's limit. Beyond is miracle.
Return imagination to the sphere, the wave four had stilled:
Golden section, curling vine, petals, starfish,
Undulant and dancing sea-born fluent

FIVE

Love would end there.
But in rest knows the cold descent of rule,
More than quadrate order where all waters close,
Lost to love and play, tyranny of bees
The radial crystal

SIX

From that ice cage
We reach out any way. Numbers
Infinite: seven music's prime, closed in the octagon,
The gods' ennead nine, three threes
And one, Gothic

TEN

Endecasyllable
Hourly market dozen and the haunted
Gulf thirteen... But all of them born of Pythagorean five
By the breeding on female two of male
And numberless

ONE

IV

The Number of My Loves

1

I have one love in the city of Florence.
When we were young we might have married;
But our language was not sufficient
For us to come to terms with each other.

How could I tell her:
"If you love me recklessly now,
You will have me for as long as husband."
Or if I had? Florence lives by custom.

That bargain was made with another. Platonic
Love is rare and not always rewarding;
But for twenty years, like brother and sister,
My Florentine and I have gone on loving.

She runs the mansion and sees to her parents.
Only at evening when the flower looks westward,
She climbs the balcony and takes the blazon
Of towers singing in the cypress valley.

And once in five years, say, I come to that city;
I kiss my Florentine and escort her on the river.
She is beautiful in face and language.
We canoe among the rocks.

I think she hardly braves the sun but then.
"You know," she says, "once in so many years,
From around the world you come like Perseus, *caro*,
And stay a day—to take me boating on the Arno."

2

Of my dark love I have told enough already;
But how should dark withdraw into its darkness
While the night flashes with intrinsic fire?

One can suffer years and learn little.
What I learned came afterwards and looking back:
That hate and love are one; that love burns forests;

That lightning kindles what the cloud-dark rain
Balanced in slow love against love's burning;
That these are poles of being: leaf and flame—

For which there are times and seasons. I have learned
We are herdsmen now and harvesters, not hunters.
It is not profitable to burn the grain

To singe a few rabbits and call it tragedy.
Do you remember when those first affairs wounded
Us and others—Europe under fire?

No skill masters the labyrinth
Of hate coiled into good. The walled garden
Wilts with blessing; burned-off barrens

Mantle with wild roses. Yet who but
The spendthrift of a jaded age would put
A torch to the world on a chance of flowers?

Must we, in love's plurality, still swear
By that star-brand ripping a sky of thunder?—
"No matter what's lost or destroyed, I want you to suffer."

3

There are loves of fact and loves of imagination.
I have been blessed all my life in the love of women.

I will praise loves like angels who kiss entire,

Mingle body and soul and unpossessing

Drift apart like clouds, break bread of passion
In charity of flesh, not promiscuity.

I could wish for loves in every part of the world,
And be a traveling salesman hawking pleasure:

Look, I have fall days here; I have spring flowers;
Limestone ledges and the limbs of swimming;

Wheat is golden in the palm of my hand;
And the shade of beechwood slumbers on my belly.

You who are queen of silence will come without calling;
We will go into the night, hierophants of nature;

And all our sounds as we are poured into each other
Will be like birds and waters, lappings, sighs;

And you will sleep, and wake filled with a secret,
That love is a drop that lingers to its pool.

You will not mind our coming or our going,
Any more than dreams, or the drift of wings or seasons;

You will get up smiling for the event of day,
And at night, holding another:

"Let him take me again when he passes this country;
Meanwhile, what is love but a gain?"

4

And there is the wife of my heart, for whom I regret
None of the other chances; for when I return
From my travels, she takes me in the kind

Arms of her wreathing, and I look into eyes
That have no shadow in them.

Like a mountain lake she is a good place
To bathe in on a sky-blue day, or drink
At the rock shore of every evening;
She is a cabin built high in the forest,
In wilderness, a fragrant house of balsam.

Our children laugh in the doorways; she is all
Neatness; she rules with order. And when I am off
On my wanderings, she writes in her brave small
Hand, my hearth's keeper: "We had Chinese
Cookies for supper with fortunes in them;

I took one for you. It said: 'Make use
Of every moment.' And for me: 'This is
A night for love and affection.' Come soon."
Sometimes I wake under the moon or stars,
As now when Venus is comforting the east,

And think my loves before me.
I am one who has been greatly favored—
Most in her, to whom I send this greeting,
May she keep her fortune a day or two, not doubting:

5

Love will come home, again and again, forever.

16

Moss-Green

Far in the spruce wood, through the stained
Twilight over the needled ground,
A space opens, as under water, brimmed
With sky and green, where a spruce tree has died.

To stretch out on the cinquefoil of that ground:
Wood sorrel, bunchberry, goldthread,
A walnut gnawed, a robin's egg,
Coil of a snail, gray feather of a dove.

Child of death, come with me
Over the brown-stained ground
To the round place of birth,
Love-luminous, moss-green.

Post coitum non tristis

And when we have done:
The loved form
Stretched on the world-floor
The round O flared
Parted lips
Speechless with adoration. . .

Phosphorescent Bay

The wake lightens; fish scatter
Like stars; painlessly
I dip my hand in flame. . .
Our youngest daughter nestles to us tired.

Venus trails in the west; I call
Its name: "A world like ours." She looks

And sighs. "And each of those Seven Sisters
Is a sun." Her eyelids fall.

The boat comes round—home
Over darkened water. Dying fires
Shine from islands where night fishermen are.
The small soul we cling to sleeps in my arms.

On Telegraph Avenue

When you were love's towhead I was the father.
The breakup hurt you worse than the others.

Years I was God in the garden: "Beware the fruit"—
Your brown eyes hungry for love and for death.

Child-marriage, heart's ease of trust and children,
Mistrusted, loosed you to the cauldron

Of Fillmore and drugs. I preached salvation
After the moral mouthings of our nation.

Dysecology and war have silenced that:
Global wrong the fruit of righteous right.

Take your guitar; sing the songs of loss.
Mind dissolves in the sway of the voice.

Crazy Jane of blues and rage,
Wrapped in a halo of heroin and rags—

I crash your spitty pavement, schooled
By the queen of the most broken street in the world.

Midsummer Night in Aspen Meadows

Winding down three valleys from fir mountains,
Converging pastures, flickering fires in dark now—
I see the world like that: multi-dimensional
Comet-slug, shaping time-space lendings as it goes.

And by each eye of fire, in the cave of Nativity,
Krishna dancers, bongo hippies, single acid brooder,
Spin cocoons of vision, inwardness as always
Reaching out—to be the whole earth-river,

Glacier of merging soul-fires down black mountains,
The comet filled with eyes, it cannot be—and is.

17

To Galway

I dreamed of you tonight, your liver
Doubling you up like a shrimp in bed.
I waked, the Yaddo scritch-owl
At it on the sill. Death-devoted
Singer—you, not that damned bird—
Something more than poet, a man:
For God's sake, mind yourself.
You are too sole to leave us here
Among so many cruds, the worse alone.

Last Supper

I taught him first. Years after, in another place,
Lay with his wife, beautiful, proffered, theirs asleep;
He, intern, hunting acid and like-sex. No hope,
No ease blessed the divided search. She told, of course;
Took the prick for that. Later, in another house,
He, doctor, knocked at midnight, mine (and wife) asleep—
To expose the teacher-false-friend who broke him up.
"We tried love and failed; your move," I said. He passed.

Lean and bearded, children, ex-wife, joint loves, hers
And his, camping in communes, dispensing medicine
For rip-off welfare, they stop. He cites Kennedy,
Test case: to praise the shot that did false promise in.
At table his eyes find mine; in mine the saint face blurs.
Crushed to mystic squalor, he loves and praises me.

Gilbert-Swamp-Blackbird

Squall. "That fatal and perfidious bark"—a canoe
Built by the wife's father for himself alone, sunk
To the gunnels, wobbly as quicksilver—what should I
Care?—having with me again our master painter, neglected
Don Quixote of the brush. Mopping water from the bottom,
My shirt for a sponge, we came, as rain cleared,
To the overgrown creek's end: beneath a rock-oak slope
And flanked with pine, a blue-green swamp of reeds, tide-
Flat surface hatched with alizarin dead stems. Across
From the crabber's shacks and long sleek boats, by a bridge
Some quirk of decay strips to the heirloom of a Chinese
Pen (where a redwing blackbird flies from the swamp nest,
Creaks like a hinge that opens into music, rupture of gold
And vermeil from black flight and the spilled rush of the trill),
We gain the wooded shore. The painter squints for a focus;
I withdrawn to a hummock of moss, lean against a pine
And write—nothing to celebrate but the fact of sharing
Again the thunder- and sky-reflecting tide-swamp world
That is ours, and the rusty creaking of a coal-black bird
That flying breaks in wings of flame and—yes—song.

Bicentennial at Hall's Restaurant

Shore up this place—old bar by the waterfront,
Copper spit-trough like a urinal,
Gilt and steamboat gothic—patch it all;
Fix the back stair senators would mount,
After state gambling, for a venal cunt;
Spot the old picture on the facing wall:
Eve sluiced out, Adam up from the Fall,
Pounding his clutched head, vain penitent.

Exhume all trust-betrayers who like him
Cursed losses here, feared what else acquired.
Subpoena dead and living to this bar:—
Now charge them: "Swill and spill! enact the dream
That leaves a screwed-out planet, pimped and hired
By Johnson, Nixon, Ford, and worse, and more!"

Winter Cave

Starnbergersee, a fourth remove, ice from the eaves,
Snow banked from the lake almost to the double panes;
Heart driven back to a stove-center,
Pursues the prayerful quest of images:
"Be like an arctic whale wrapped in its blubber."

That fall and winter in the shack at the dunes,
After the lost elections, the old painter
Gilbert, fierce poet Kinnell, and Bell
(Prophet verse betrayed) heaped the chunk-stove,
Chicago far off lowering through its cloud.

When the first blizzard flung the waves in crystal,
We almost lost the insular illusion.
That night, from shook bedding, lamplit dust
Wheeled and melted south: external wind
Blew through the clapboard space a horn of judgment. . .

Death on a bulldozer follows after. . .
Until this other stove-room windows Now:
Ours the wilderness beyond the city,
Along the lake that signifies all water—
Three gathered in one loss, past overthrow.

18

March Snow

My love is out of town
And the March snow
Like grit bevels around
The four-quartered windows
Of the tower.

I dream of a spring bank
Where moss revives
Earth's precursive
First attempt
At flowers.

Not likely,
Dream being free,
A man would stretch out
Alone, under the conceptual
Beech tree.

While the horizon tilts white planes,
Traveler, I give you leave;
But come with the thaw:—
Our flower-rites
Ask flesh not dream.

Neighborly

She's like an apple tree
that leans
over the wall;

She belongs to him
but her fruits fall
to me.

Moonrise

I rise and climb the dunes. A waning moon
Breaks over an ocean shore it washes clean.
I am content in the ruins of nakedness.

Sleeping or waking, listen, all I have loved:

The heart of an old man wants nothing more
When the dead moon spills its yellow seed
In the heaving and sighing salt furrows of the sea.

Late

The earth still has trees
Green-leaved against
The blue of day,
Stirred at night over stars—
Poignancies.

I dream earth tonight,
Its soul-pool round it
Like a swarm of bees
Darting in for birth,
Taught by us displaced
The crisis of the hive. . .

I wake wide of the mark.
Impossible the spaces
For another start.

Speculum Mundi

Light through cloud now poured from the spent sun
Receiver I to the childing of your touch
I who next will be the very light
Poured down cloud for the receiver eye
Great either way sight cloud and sun
You into me with the same spending touch
As I then into you with child by my light.

19

Libations

Is it now at last beginning, the wonderful
Slow night of embered radiance, when the powers
That warm their evenings at our hearts
Take the good of the fire, sit down in love
And holy drunkenness, and pour on us
Libations to the quiet above the gods?

Wedding Dance

Strobe light green: trumpets, drums;
Hips flared, crotch front flung;
Red light: tuck twat, snaked up arms.
No fuck, fuck-dance; stab-light green;
Rum-tuckers, strobe strutters, old on young.
Hey old mother-rutter, rub a tub o' bubs;
Stoke that trombone.
Fuck-dance, daughter, shake your little thing.
Plug a bugger, gap-face, ruck that drum;
Plump those strings.
Green tongue, red prong, long-haired balls;
Follow your guts and strut your holes.
Gong it solo, boom to boom.
No fuck, fuck-dance; beat my strobe;
Suckers and whuckers are flesh of God.
Red bang—green bang—horn hot hole:
One God-swot in the all-God whole.

Third World

In the burning selva waiting weeks for rain,
When the sky clouds over and wind comes in gusts,
Under the forest tent you hear a mournful rustle;
It is leaves, not drops, leaves of the rainless
Winter, that fall from the terraced roof.
And you wait in a smoky wood where fire creeps through the brush,
Listen for the sound to change, from dry to a liquid spill—
Globed water gurgling to rain-forest rivers green and full.

Lean to the Ponderosa

This landscape, roll with it; flow out over lava
Mesas, first smog creeping from Albuquerque
And over the Chama gap from Farmington;

This landscape that was fire and will be smoke-
Poison (we agar-plate bacteria), feel now
Its soul in the rock, springs in the rivers;

In the basalt bowl lifted over the world, sit
And wait chastened; not hate. . . not even pity;
Wonder at a being whose fatal flaw was love.

Wallberg Lift

From the cloud of Munich in a bubble chair
We reach a height where it is autumn clear;
Stripped on crystal cobbles in bright air,
Dream the garden aether of beginning.
Wake—to muffled music: organ, choir,
And faint as under water lost bells ringing.
From dim churches and mist-vaulted towers
In the passion valley of our homing
We take the Lethe of the vesper hours.
Tears plant flesh upon us. Great with longing
We sink in darkness toward the fallen singing.

[69]

20

What Love Shapes

Wishing a presence time and space withhold,
I walk the twilight of a settled road;
Far off, one appears; I call the name,
Start forward to a likeness which is dream.

Three hundred years of seeing still rehearse
The Cartesian axioms of the universe.

An arbor on a hill behind a house,
A cesspool under, winter odorous;
Remembering vintages I dwell on shapes
Of frost-brown vines: what I smell is grapes.

How often with others have you closed your eyes,
Felt their being in you, and known it mine?

Deirdre

By the Roman fable, for perfect luxury,
The sum of the ages should be seventy.

Beautiful married women, blown and mellow,
How that doctrine cheered a wandering scholar;

Cheered from year to year an aging tutor,
Playing for younger nymphs Silenus satyr.

Seventy nears; I think with reluctance
Of old Tiberius and his infant sucklings.

Deirdre, youngest, warmest, all accurve,
You're too old for me—forget it, and let's love.

Lake-Dusk-Pines-Moon

The water holds the brown sky of dusk.
Who set that little fire by the lake?
Who let the twilight through the pines
Fold this crescent sliver of a moon?
Who made dimensionality ambiguous,
Eye's mirror-lake of pines, dusk and moon?

Charm for a Sick Planet

Fill the god pots with god-brew:—

Call Truth the spinner of the world—
The dying need it, the new-born need it;
Hold it together as long as you can.

We who tore the earth-robe
Crying still the birth of God,
Gather at the spring of paradox.

Motion is its own, not for a goal:
The jet of time in the pool of now.
"I am" speaks the gravity of stone;

"I am", the levity of wind;
"I am", the rip-saw of fire;
"I am" laps water as it flows.

Think water, fire, air, earth will hold
On the sun-terraces of the world
(As long as they can) rebellious soul:—

Then spill the god-pots to the ground.

Complins of Youth and Age

From earth hung in space, as from a ship
Heeled to the blue gulf rayed with light—
Mutined, cannoned, bloodied, tongued with burning—
Repeat the hymn of the first evening earth:

How the round pearl of a world mothered in air
Falls quietly turning; and our evening falls. . .
Fields of wheat or barley, standing or
In swaths, or shocks like random trees, and trees
That close the fields in somber sheaves—fuse
A complin music down the depths and shoals
Of the atom-weaving, spirit-breathing worlds. . .

If oneness with all-ocean cannot save
The ship mind overreached, it may seed starry space.
Where the spent light-bearer spreads his arms,
Himself the flesh he nails, the cruciform earth-shadow,
Down and down, sounds through the complin wave:
"Fathering fire, forgive; mothering void, receive!"

V

Water-Fire-Air-Earth-Void

1   Birth by WATER always, liquid love:
You have seen oceans moving, tides and waves
That leap at breaking and are air, cloud-foam,
Then drops, whole-seeking rounds, each hungry
For the next, quick-silver joined; from space
How green all globe an earth sun-glanced,
A bay at evening, where the level rays
Bleed amber through the blue concaves;
So love refracts in your translucent mould
And turns its ash, breath, moisture into fire.

2   The cosmic masses are not earth but FIRE, kindled
In void, space-crystals gone to liquid, vapor, heat;
Until the plunge is stayed, a stilled blaze—

    Plus and minus balanced into dance, fondled
In passion, as the groove and spool of rutting tame
The Deirdre flame: loins for all asplay, the red lance

    Reared for all: as I with you, you whet for me
The craze of flesh, lust-gorging ways—
Dandled at the faithful hearth of play.

3   Stilled almost to the ambience of AIR,
Almost beyond its nature,

    As clouds at sunset,
Even of thunder, fold to the light

    Rapt limbs of pleasure
Wind-caressed, or water laves a shore

    Or thought pervades the limestone of a land
Held in all its breathings, sight and sound.

4 What is this EARTH-concretion Dante spread, a last
  Periphery of the point of fire, as basalt crusts
  On lava, salt from seas? Genesis could only risk
  Fall by freedom, nature the destruct of quest.
  As Leonardo in a mottled wall, we trace
  In schist the stilled orogeny of every earth.

5 Maelstroms of light, black holes, star-sinks in space;
  VOID only chambers the death-birth of all;
  Fire, air, earth and water, act and word
  Mirage from the zero-flexings of all void:
  To hold that calm and aching mothers god.